THE SPROUT FAIRIES

Forever Fairies

Lulu Flutters

MADDY MARA
Author of
Dragon Girls

By Maddy Mara

Forever Fairies

Dragon Girls

Dragon Games

THE SPROUT FAIRIES

Forever Fairies

Lulu Flutters

by Maddy Mara

Scholastic Inc.

ISBN 978-1-339-00119-7

10 9 8 7 6 5 4 3 2 1   24 25 26 27 28

Printed in the U.S.A.   40

First printing 2024

Book design by Cassy Price

It was the first day of spring and magic was in the air. In a little glade within a vast forest, four flowers swayed in the breeze: a daffodil, a tulip, a poppy, and a lily. The flowers were waiting for the sun to rise. Slowly, the pink-and-gold dawn melted across the sky.

The first flower touched by the morning light was the daffodil. Its petals began to open, filling the air with a gentle scent. Curled inside was a tiny fairy. She had honey-brown hair with a bright blue streak in it, and long eyelashes. The fairy was wearing a little yellow dress. Her wings were folded neatly against her back.

The daffodil wobbled gently. "Wake up, Lulu," the flower murmured. "It's your Sprout Day!"

The little fairy opened one eye and then the other. She sat up and looked around. So *this* was the world! Lulu's flower had been whispering stories and singing songs into her dreams as she grew. Finally, Lulu could see it all for herself. See it *and* explore it!

Lulu fluttered her wings. It felt good to stretch them. She had been curled up inside her flower for a long time. Her wings were twitching to go.

The daffodil's sweet words filled the air. "Before you try out your wings, take a sip of flower nectar. You'll need the energy."

A drop of nectar glimmered on the petal like a pearl. Lulu reached up and caught it in her tiny hands. It tasted like sunshine. Energy raced through her. Now she was ready to fly!

Lulu had never flown before—after all, she had only

just sprouted. But with a couple of quick flaps, she zoomed into the air and hovered above her flower.

"Good work, Lulu!" the daffodil sang. "Go higher! I'll catch you if you fall."

Lulu rose until she could see all the flowers in the glade. Were there any other fairies about to sprout? She really, *really* hoped she wasn't the only one sprouting today. Exploring with others would be much more fun!

The sun had just reached the tulip. As Lulu watched, its purple petals opened. Lulu could feel in her wings that something wonderful was about to happen.

A little face peered around a petal. This fairy

had velvety dark curls with purple streaks, and big brown eyes. She was wearing a cute little hat and a purple dress.

"Happy Sprout Day!" Lulu called, fluttering over to the tulip. "I'm Lulu. I just sprouted, too."

The fairy smiled. "Happy Sprout Day to you!" she said. "I'm Nova. Is flying fun?" Just then, a gust of wind blew the fairy's hat off her head and into the air.

In a flash, Lulu darted after the hat and caught it easily. She handed it back to Nova. "Flying is so much fun. And it's useful for rescuing hats! Come and try it."

First, Nova took a sip of nectar from her tulip.

Then she flapped her wings, rising up to hover beside Lulu.

"See that big poppy?" Lulu pointed. "I have a feeling there's another fairy inside!"

Lulu and Nova watched closely. As soon as the sun touched the poppy, it unfurled. The red petals twinkled in the gentle light.

Sure enough, another fairy was sitting cross-legged at the poppy's center. She was wearing bright red. Her hair, glossy black with gold streaks, fell across her shoulders.

"Happy Sprout Day!" Lulu and Nova sang together.

A smiled blossomed on the fairy's little face. "Thanks! I'm Coco. Who are you?"

"This is Nova," Lulu said, pointing at Nova.

"And that's Lulu," Nova said, pointing at Lulu. "Take a sip of flower nectar, then come join us!"

Coco drank thirstily. Then she shook out her wings and launched into the air. "Where's the fourth fairy?" Coco asked. "My flower said there were four of us sprouting today."

Lulu looked around. At the edge of the glade was a huge lily plant. Upon it grew a single pale pink bud. "I think she's on her way!" Lulu said, excited.

The morning sun touched the lily. The flower

gave a little shake and the petals opened. The fairies watched with big eyes.

But no fairy appeared!

Lulu, Nova, and Coco looked at one another. *What was going on?*

"Let's go and see," Lulu suggested.

Lulu zipped over to the flower. Nova and Coco were not far behind. They peeped in. Lying inside the lily, fast asleep, was the fourth fairy. She had wavy pale hair streaked with pink, the same color as her dress. And this fairy was the tiniest of them all!

"What's that sound?" Nova asked, looking around. "Is it a bee buzzing?"

Coco burst out laughing. "She's snoring! How can such a big noise come from such a tiny thing?"

The lily gave a little shake. But the sleeping fairy kept on snoring.

Lulu, Nova, and Coco grinned at one another.

"HAPPY SPROUT DAY!" the three fairies sang at the top of their lungs.

The final fairy stretched and yawned. Her eyes blinked open. When she saw three faces looking down at her, she sat up. "Good morning! I'm Zali. You must be Lulu, Nova, and Coco. My flower's sleeping song was all about you."

Zali scooped up some nectar from her lily, drank deeply, and then spread her tiny wings and rose out of her flower to join the others. "It's great to finally meet you! I wonder what happens now?"

The sound of fluttering made the four fairies look up. Another fairy was flying toward them—very, very quickly! She was bigger than

Lulu and the others, and had a long ponytail streaked with blue. Her sleek blue outfit had a stripe of yellow down one leg and an *A* embroidered on the front. The fairy did a neat loop in the air and came to a stop.

I'm going to learn how to fly like that, Lulu thought.

"Welcome to the Magic Forest, little Sprout Wings!" the fairy called.

Lulu, Coco, Nova, and Zali clustered around the
bigger fairy. They all began talking at once.

"Hi! What's your name?"

"What do we do next?"

"How did you know we were here?"

"Are we going to fly somewhere?"

The bigger fairy put up her hands and laughed. "Slow down, Sprouties! You'll find out much more if you let me speak."

The little fairies fell silent. Their wings shimmered in the morning light.

"My name is Etta," said the fairy, flicking back her ponytail. "And I'm here to bring you to the Forever Tree."

Lulu's daffodil had told her about the Forever Tree. The Forever Fairies all lived within its branches. Lulu could hardly wait to see it!

The Sprout Wings had a thousand more questions.

"How far away is it?"

"Do you live there?"

"What happens when we arrive?"

"Can we go there right now?"

Etta laughed again, shaking her head in wonder. "You are the most excited Sprouties I've ever met. I'll explain on the way. But first, zip over to those white flowers and back. We have a long journey ahead. I need to see how well you can fly."

The four little fairies fluttered across the glade toward the white flowers. Lulu was in front. She just loved flying! With each flap of her wings, she surged through the air, faster and faster.

As Lulu neared the white flowers, she saw a

bug sparkling in the sunlight—and it was about to fall off a petal! Lulu swooshed over and caught the bug in her arms. "I've got you!" She popped it safely onto a bigger petal and kept flying. Lulu was going so fast she almost crashed into Coco, Nova, and Zali coming the other way. "Sorry!" she called.

"Wow! You're so speedy!" Nova said.

"Wait for us!" Coco laughed.

Lulu hadn't realized how far ahead she was. The funny thing was, she didn't feel like she'd been trying very hard.

When Lulu returned, Etta smiled. "Good flying. And that was a nice rescue. Sparklebugs can be so clumsy! Let me guess, you had lots of flying dreams when you were growing in your flower?"

"I did!" Lulu said. "But it's even better in real life."

Etta nodded. "You and I are alike."

Lulu beamed. She loved the idea of being like this fast, cool fairy.

Soon, Nova, Coco, and Zali joined them, panting but happy.

"Was that okay?" Zali puffed. "We're not as fast as Lulu. She's amazing!"

Lulu felt a flash of worry. Should she have slowed down? She didn't want the others to think she was showing off. She already liked the other Sprout Wings, and she wanted them to like her back!

"You all did wonderfully," Etta said. "Sprouties usually take a while to get the hang of flying. But you four are naturals."

"Shall we go?" Coco asked. "I can't wait to see the Forever Tree."

"I like your enthusiasm, Coco. Yes, let's go!" Etta turned and headed for the dense thicket surrounding the glade. Coco, Nova, and Zali followed close behind.

Lulu turned to look at her daffodil one last time. It gave a bob of its yellow head. "Safe travels, Lulu. I know you'll make me proud!"

Lulu waved goodbye and sped off after the others. She caught up easily.

Etta spoke as they flew over a grove of wildflowers. "The Forever Fairies protect the forest in lots of different ways. We've done this forever—and we'll keep doing it forever! Even the oldest creatures of the forest cannot remember a time when we weren't here, helping out."

Nova looked curious. "How do we look after the forest?"

"That depends on which pod you're put into," Etta said.

"Ooh! My flower told me about the fairy pods," Coco said. "There are four different ones, right?"

"That's correct," Etta said. "There are the Flutterflies, that's my pod. Then there are the Shimmerbuds, Twinklestars, and Sparkleberries. Over the next few days, you will do a series of try-outs to discover which pod you each belong in."

Coco clapped, excited. "What do we have to do for these tryouts?"

Nova looked calm and thoughtful. "Will we be given time to practice?"

Zali was gazing off dreamily. "What's it like, being in Flutterfly?"

Lulu had a question, too. It was a big one: Could all four Sprout Wings be in the same pod?

But before Lulu could ask anything, Etta called, "Watch out, everyone!"

Etta ducked under the low-hanging branch that had appeared. Lulu did the same, followed by Coco. Nova approached next, swooping under the branch in her careful way. Lulu looked around for Zali. She was trailing behind the group, gazing around in wonder. She clearly hadn't heard Etta's warning.

In a flash, Lulu zoomed back to the tiny fairy. She grabbed Zali's hand and pulled her under the branch just in time.

"Whoops!" Zali looked frazzled. "Thanks, Lulu!"

Etta nodded at them approvingly. "It's good that you're watching out for your fellow Sprouties, Lulu."

Lulu felt a glow of pride.

They were deep in the forest now, flying between huge, mossy trees. Beams of sunshine filtered through the canopy. Lulu felt like she could fly forever. But then she glanced at the others.

Nova's wings were looking a little droopy. So were Coco's and Zali's.

I'll help them out, Lulu decided. She looped up and over the group so that she was behind them. She started flapping the air with her wings to push the other fairies along. But instead of helping, Lulu's gusts of wind tossed the little fairies in all directions. Nova's hat got caught in Zali's long hair, and Coco was flipped upside down.

"Oops! Sorry!" cried Lulu.

But everyone just laughed as they straightened themselves out.

"That was a good thought, Lulu," Etta said. "The Turbo Boost is a very complex Flutterfly move, and you nearly nailed it. I'll teach you how to perfect it someday. But don't worry, we're almost at the tree now. We just need to get through those brambles."

Up ahead was a twisted snarl of vines studded with thorns. Lulu could just make out a few narrow tunnels through the tangle.

"Follow me," Etta called cheerfully. "But don't get hooked on the thorns!" She disappeared into the brambles. After a moment's hesitation, Coco followed.

"Here goes," muttered Nova, flying through a little slower.

Lulu knew she could zip through the brambles

easily. But then she looked at Zali. Her face was very pale.

"Let's go through together," Lulu suggested.

Linking arms, the two fairies squeezed through the gap, nipping under one vine and around another, avoiding all the sharp thorns.

A moment later, Lulu and Zali burst through the brambles. Waiting for them on the other side was the most incredible sight.

An enormous tree loomed before them. Its mossy

trunk was as wide as three normal trees. It was

so tall, Lulu couldn't see the top! Countless little

windows were dotted along the sturdy branches.

At the base of the trunk was a grand door, golden

and etched with swirling patterns.

Lulu gasped. "The Forever Tree!"

"It's just how I imagined." Coco sighed.

Nova nodded, her eyes sparkling. Zali simply stared.

As they watched, the Forever Tree gave a dramatic shake...and burst into bloom! In an instant, the branches were covered in flowers of every color imaginable.

"Come on, Sprouties!" Etta cried, hovering near the huge trunk. "The other fairies are waiting."

The four Sprout Wings looked at one another, confused. *What other fairies?*

There was the sound of tinkling bells and the

front door flung open. A stream of fairies poured out and surged into the air, cheering loudly. More fairies squeezed out of the windows, flitting here and there in the golden sunlight.

There were boy fairies and girl fairies, tall fairies and short fairies. Fairies with long raven-black hair and fairies with short purple hair. Some of the fairies were around Etta's age, and others were only a bit bigger than the Sprout Wings. All the fairies were dressed in colorful outfits. And all of them were chattering with excitement.

"The new Sprouties are here!"

"Look how cute they are!"

"So tiny! They still have pollen on their wings."

Etta flew to the front of the crowd. "Flutter back, everyone!" Her voice rang out clear and firm. "Give our new Sprout Wings some space. Remember what it felt like on your first day."

The fairies moved back, but Lulu still felt

self-conscious. She'd never had so many eyes on her! Zali pressed close, clearly feeling the same.

"Where are the other Alpha Wings?" Etta called to the crowd.

"What are Alpha Wings again?" Coco asked the other Sprouties.

"They're like the head fairies," Nova explained. "I think there's one for each pod."

"We're coming!" came a friendly voice. "Make way, please."

The crowd parted and three fairies joined Etta. They looked like they were all about the same age. They each had an *A* for *Alpha* on their chests, just like Etta.

The Alphas were all dressed differently. One wore a shimmery skirt made of deep green leaves with a purple petal top. Another was wearing a silver dress, shaped like a bell and pulled tight with a golden sash. She had lights in her hair. The third fairy wore a long dusty-pink-and-aqua dress covered in flowing ruffles.

Lulu stared at them in awe. They looked so amazing!

Etta caught her eye and winked. "Don't be intimidated by the Alphas. We were once little Sprout Wings like you. In fact, we four sprouted together." Etta turned to the fairy in the silver bell dress. "Do you remember our first day, Timi?"

"Of course! Vida and I crashed into each other just as all the other fairies came out of the tree," Timi said, grabbing the hand of the fairy in the leafy skirt.

"It was worse for Mave." Vida gave the elegant fairy in the long ruffly dress a teasing smile.

Mave groaned. "Don't remind me." She turned to the Sprout Wings. "I was so stunned by the Forever Tree that I totally forgot to flap my wings. I fell straight into a puddle. I had to meet everyone for the first time dripping in mud!"

Everyone laughed, and Lulu relaxed. These big fairies didn't seem scary now that she could picture them making mistakes.

Coco put up a hand. "I have a question," she said. "When do we start the tryouts?"

"Tomorrow," Etta said. "First, we need to grow you a room. You four will stay together until the Pod Picking, which happens after all the tryouts are completed."

Lulu, Nova, Coco, and Zali huddled together and squealed in delight.

"Did you say *grow* us a room?" Zali asked.

Timi smiled. "Watch! Fairies, please move away from the tree."

Like a fluttery, multicolored cloud, the fairies flew to the edges of the clearing. The four Alpha Wings gathered before the majestic tree, their wings flapping in unison. Each Alpha pulled out a shimmering silver wand from their belt. Together, they lifted their wands high and began to make beautiful, complicated shapes in the air.

Lulu felt a buzz of excitement. Beams of glittery color flowed out of the wands, each of a different hue. The glittering trails spread until they wrapped all around the massive tree.

A tiny shoot began growing out of the tree's trunk. It was the bright green of fresh growth. Waving back and forth, the new shoot became bigger and bigger. Darker leaves and flower buds sprouted forth. Soon, the shoot was nearly as big as the other branches!

"Can I do the windows?" the Alpha called Vida asked. "That's my favorite part."

The other Alphas nodded. Vida gave her wand a sharp flick, sending a stream of pink magic swooshing over to the new branch. Little curtained windows popped up along its length.

"Perfect, Vida!" Etta turned to Lulu and the others. "Want to see inside your new home?"

It was a silly question. Of course they did!

"This way!" Etta flew toward the main entrance.

"And don't forget to change your shoes!"

At the golden door, Etta hovered above a little

patch of purple moss. There was a puff of sparkly

dust, and Etta's outdoor shoes transformed into

little slippers. One by one, the other Sprout Wings

paused above the moss. The sparkly dust tickled Lulu's feet! Admiring her soft slippers, Lulu followed Etta and the others inside. A stream of other fairies flew in behind them, still chattering away as slippers magically appeared on their tiny feet.

Inside was a huge, dimly lit hall. There was just enough light for the fairies to see the mosaic of gleaming, twinkling stones that covered the floor.

"My flower said this floor is made of a thousand gemstones from every corner of the Magic Forest," Zali said.

Etta nodded. "And the pattern changes to match

what's happening for the Forever Fairies." Next, Etta looked upward. "Hi, bees! Lights, please!"

Instantly, the hall was flooded with warm light. A faint scent of honey filled the room.

"Are they glow bees?" Nova asked, gazing at the moving orbs of light above.

"Yes! The glow bees live in a nearby hive," Etta explained. "Every day, a group of them comes here and provides us with light. In return, the Shimmerbud fairies nurse them when they're ill. The creatures of the forest all help one another when they can."

Now that the lights were on, Lulu saw that countless staircases were carved into the tree.

They curved up and around until they disappeared
out of view. Little doors were dotted here and
there, leading to all the different branches.

Four glow bees flew closer to the Sprout Wings,
their fluffy bodies pulsing with comforting light.

"Ah! Here are your bee guides," Etta said. "They
will show you to your sleeping branch, where
you'll find everything you need. I know this is all

really exciting, but try to have a nap. You'll need all your energy for the Flutterfly tryout tomorrow."

Lulu's stomach swirled. She didn't know if it was from excitement or nerves! She had a feeling she would like being a Flutterfly. "What sort of fairies become Flutterflies?" she asked.

"Well, we're the sporty fairies," Etta explained. "We are fast, and we use our flying and acrobatic skills to help the forest's creatures. For example, if an animal is trapped by a falling tree or stuck in a flood, we're the first on the scene."

Flying around the forest helping others sounded great to Lulu!

"But being a Flutterfly isn't all serious." Etta did

an elegant midair backflip as she went on. "We also organize the Fairy Games!"

Coco raised a hand eagerly. "What do we have to do for the Flutterfly tryout?"

"Good question. It's an adventure course. You'll have to fly fast and do stunts, too. It's the best way for the judges to see if you have the right skills to be a Flutterfly. It's fun, but it's not easy!" As she was talking, Etta had stepped into a handstand.

Lulu wanted to learn how to do that, too!

There was a sudden chiming of bells. Etta flipped back up. "Gotta go!" she called cheerfully, heading for the door. "I have to help set up the course. Remember, take a nap!"

"This way, Sprout Wings," buzzed the glow bees in unison. They flew toward the staircase. "Please note there is no flying on the stairs—unless you're a glow bee."

Lulu and the others dropped to the ground and tucked in their wings. They hurried to follow the bees. There were a lot of stairs to climb. Luckily, they were wonderful to walk on. Each step made a soft musical tone! Lulu was almost sorry when the bees stopped a few flights up. They were standing in front of a green door with a little golden knob.

"This leads to your Sprout Wings branch," the bees buzzed. "Go on!"

Coco opened the door and the Sprout Wings

burst through. The glow bees followed, taking up position near the ceiling. The branch filled with their soft glimmer as the door swung closed.

The walls of the sleeping branch were polished and smooth, like in the entrance hall. But the wood here was pale, with the fresh smell of new growth. Along one side were four windows, with a bed below each. The beds were plump with pillows and cozy coverlets made from petals. One was made from daffodils, another from purple tulips. The third was made from poppies and the last from pink lilies.

"They match our sprout flowers!" Lulu sighed

happily, running her hand over the daffodil coverlet. Her name was written in curling golden letters on the headboard.

"Look! We each have a suitcase," Nova said, admiring a tiny case made from a walnut shell. "I wonder what's inside."

"Lots of things!" Coco had already opened hers. "There's a nightdress, a toothbrush, and some fluffy socks."

"And this must be for the tryout tomorrow." Lulu held up a blue-and-yellow flying suit just like the one Etta wore. The only difference was Lulu's had an *S* embroidered on the front.

"*S* for *Sprout Wing*!" Coco sang, admiring her suit.

Lulu looked closely at hers. "I don't think this is going to fit me—the legs are too short."

"Me neither!" Zali held her enormous costume against her tiny frame.

"Let's try them on," Nova suggested. "I have a feeling it will work out."

Lulu nodded. Nova didn't say much—but when she did, she was usually right! Lulu pulled off her daffodil sprouting dress and stepped into the stretchy blue-and-yellow suit. As she did, the material shifted and changed to fit her body. Soon, it was a perfect fit. Lulu immediately felt comfy and sporty, like she was ready to fly anywhere.

She looked at the others. Their costumes were also adjusting to fit. The Sprouties twisted this way and that, enjoying their new flying suits.

"Don't forget to nap," buzzed the glow bees from above.

"I don't feel like napping," Coco admitted.

Neither did Lulu. She was wide-awake and still full of flower nectar energy.

"We *could* nap," Zali said, smiling mischievously. "Or we could practice for the Flutterfly tryout."

Lulu liked this idea!

To her surprise, the glow bees hummed approvingly. "That's what we would do," they buzzed. "Why waste time sleeping when you could be bizzzzy?"

Nova nodded. "But how do we practice?"

"Like this!" Zali sprang onto her bed and began

jumping up and down, fluttering her tiny wings to go higher, and then tucking them in tight to fall faster.

Soon, all four fairies were leaping and flying and tumbling from one bed to another. Pillows and petal coverlets flew in every direction. Lulu jumped so high she touched the ceiling!

"Why do the new Sprout Wings *always* jump on the beds?" Lulu heard one glow bee ask another.

Lula was about to explain how fun it was when she caught sight of something out the window. She stopped mid-jump and yelped in surprise.

The other Sprout Wings stopped jumping, too.

"What is it?" Coco asked.

Lulu pointed. "I just saw two faces peeping in the window! But they vanished when they saw me looking."

"Maybe it was some bigger fairies?" Zali said. "They seem pretty interested in us."

Lulu shook her head. "They were green. And they didn't have wings."

"No wings?" Nova's eyes were wide. "How did they get up so high?"

"I think they were dangling from ropes." Lulu was starting to wonder if she'd imagined the whole thing. But no! She had definitely seen two green faces. They had grinned at her. And one of them had crossed their eyes in a very rude way!

"Sounds like trolls," said the glow bees from

above. "They're extremely curious. They're always buzzing around our hive—they love our honey."

"Are trolls good?" Lulu asked the glow bees. "Or are they bad?"

"Neither," buzzed two of the bees.

"Both," buzzed the other two at the same time.

The Sprout Wings looked at one another. That was not very helpful!

"No more questions, Sprout Wings. Etta is about to knock," the bees declared.

Sure enough, there was a friendly rap on the door and Etta walked in—on her hands.

The Sprout Wings burst out laughing. Etta

seemed to spend as much time upside down as the right way up!

Even more impressively, Etta was balancing a basket on top of her slipper-covered feet. When she reached the middle of the room, she kicked the basket into the air, flipped upright, and neatly caught it in her hands. "This is your dinner." Etta put the basket in the corner. "But before you eat, we're going on a tree tour. Everyone ready?"

First, they visited the library, a huge branch lined with rows and rows of books. Fairies lounged about on comfy cushions, reading. Lulu noticed that lots of the readers were dressed in the Shimmerbud colors of purple and green.

A flock of books fluttered over to greet the new arrivals. The books particularly liked Nova and started following her around.

"Fairy books are good at sniffing out readers," Etta told Nova. "I think you'll be popular in here."

Next, they explored the craft branch, which the Sparkleberries kept neat and well stocked with all kinds of supplies. Tiny Zali was soon lost among the bolts of fabric, brushes, and paint.

"Can I come here every day?" Zali's eyes shone as she sifted through a chest full of color-changing beads.

"Of course!" a Sparkleberry mending her

pink-and-aqua dress responded. "You can even take some things with you now, if you like."

Delighted, Zali gathered up some string and beads.

"What are you going to make?" asked Lulu.

Zali just smiled. "You'll find out!"

Finally, they visited one of the tree's many magical kitchens. Twinklestar fairies in silver aprons flittered here and there, baking and stirring, adding and tasting. It all smelled delicious! Coco kept asking questions and peering into steaming pots. She looked like she never wanted to leave.

"Okay, Sprouties—it's getting late. Are you hungry?" Etta asked.

They nodded.

"Of course you are! Sprouties are always hungry. Let's get back to your branch. I'll grow you a table where we can eat dinner."

The group traveled along narrow branches and up and down spiraling staircases all the way back to their cozy branch. There, Etta pulled out her sparkly wand. Lulu looked at it enviously. Her flower had sung to her about wands. She couldn't wait to get one herself.

Etta waved her wand in an intricate pattern, and out swirled trails of yellow and blue light. The floor of the bedroom began to shudder. A new sprout burst up like a water fountain. It twisted and grew until it was waist-high, and then flattened to form a tabletop. It even had a leafy tablecloth! With another clever swish of her wand, Etta made five little stools grow up around the table.

Next, Etta unpacked the plates, bowls, and cutlery. She unwrapped thick slices of fresh bread, spread with something golden.

"That's glow honey," the glow bees buzzed proudly. "You're lucky to be trying our latest batch."

"There's also a dash of it in the soup," Etta told the bees, pulling an acorn out of the basket and lifting off its cap. Inside was a shimmering liquid that filled the room with a delicious, sweet scent.

The four little fairies ate hungrily, if a little clumsily—none of them had used a spoon before. Lulu kept spilling soup on her flying suit.

"Anyone who thinks fairies are dainty should watch Sprout Wings eat their first bowl of soup," tutted a glow bee.

Lulu felt her face go red, but Etta chuckled. "You four are doing great. I dropped my first soup bowl on the floor! And anyway, mess-fixing spells are easy. Watch."

With a few quick, expert flicks of Etta's wand, the dishes were clean and returned to the basket, and the splodges of soup on Lulu and the other Sprout Wings vanished.

"It's not a glamorous spell," Etta said, tucking her wand back into her sleeve. "But it sure comes in handy."

Zali let out a yawn. "Sorry! Why am I so tired?"

The other three caught Zali's yawn and joined in.

Etta raised an eyebrow at the yawning Sprout Wings. "Did you four have a nap, like I suggested?"

The Sprout Wings looked at one another guiltily.

"Knew you wouldn't." Etta laughed as she tucked the basket under one arm. "But it's been a huge day, and tomorrow will be even bigger. So have an early night, yeah? And absolutely *no* leaving the tree after sunset. Sprout Wings are not allowed out after dark. Sleep tight! I'll be here early in the morning to collect you."

Etta gave them each a tender look and flew out of the room. Three glow bees followed her, leaving a single bee pulsing gently like a night-light.

As the day began to fade, the fairies changed into their nightgowns, brushed their teeth in their tiny bathroom, and climbed into their soft beds.

"It's like a cloud." Zali sighed. She fell asleep

almost immediately, as did Nova and Coco. Except for gentle fairy breathing, silence fell over the Sprout Wings' branch.

Only Lulu was awake. She kept thinking about the Flutterfly tryout tomorrow. She felt more and more certain that it was the pod for her. *But what happens if I do badly in the tryout?* she worried.

From outside came a sudden sound. Lulu slipped out of bed and fluttered to the window. She pushed it open and voices floated in. They definitely weren't fairy voices. Could they be trolls? Lulu hadn't been in the Forever Tree for long, but she already wanted to protect it. *I have to check,* she decided.

But there was one problem: Etta had told them not to leave the branch after dark, and Lulu didn't want to break the rules. But what if the trolls were up to something? Something dangerous?

She looked at the three Sprout Wings sleeping soundly. *They're my friends!* she realized suddenly. *If there's danger nearby, I need to know.*

Taking a big breath, Lulu flew out the window and into the cool night air.

It was so exciting to be out! Lulu had heard about the night sky—but it was something else to *see* it, full of stars that twinkled like gemstones.

Once again, she heard voices. Looking up through the branches, Lulu spotted two pairs of dangling legs. Green ones! Her heart was beating as quickly

as her wings, but she pushed herself to fly higher.
Finally, she came face-to-face with two creatures.
One had short, spiky hair and the other's was long
and tangled.

"Tex! Here's the fairy who saw us through the
window," said the long-haired one.

"You're right, Rox. She broke a fairy rule by
sneaking out here! I didn't think she'd be brave
enough," said the spiky-haired one.

Lulu put her hands on her hips. "Fairies are
brave! And sometimes they break the rules."

The two creatures grinned at her.

"Well said, little one," said Tex. "The best fairies
are nearly as naughty as trolls."

"So you *are* trolls!" Lulu said breathlessly.

Tex and Rox looked at each other.

"Let's see," said Rox. "Gorgeous green hair. Super powerful green legs. Adorable green snub noses. Yep, I'd say we're trolls."

The trolls laughed in a deep, earthy way that made Lulu want to join in.

"We've seen you flying. You're pretty good," Tex said, looking at Lulu. "Let me guess—you want to be a Flutterfly?"

Lulu frowned. "How did you know that?"

"Trolls just know these things." He shrugged. "The Flutterfly tryout is hard this year. Or should I say *tricky*?"

"Maybe you should say *sticky*?" Rox grinned.

The trolls found this extremely funny. But Lulu didn't! She wondered if they were planning to mess with the adventure course tomorrow. They wouldn't actually hurt her and her friends, right? "What do you mean?" she demanded.

"Let's just say, we know you're good at flying. But how good are you at *falling*?" Tex chuckled.

Before Lulu could ask what they were talking about, the trolls jumped to their broad feet. "Fairies are coming!"

"Really?" Lulu looked around. She couldn't hear anything.

"Yep. Troll hearing is better than fairy hearing."

Rox uncurled a vine from her waistband in one smooth movement. "Got to go. Good luck with the tryout tomorrow. And if anyone asks, you didn't see us!"

Rox and Tex swung on their ropes and disappeared. Then Lulu heard the flutter of wings and quiet voices. Fairies *were* nearby!

Lulu's mind was racing as she zoomed down to her window and slipped back inside. Should she wake the others? But the three fairies were still fast asleep. *I'll tell them about the trolls in the morning,* Lulu decided as she snuggled under the daffodil covers.

❀ ❀ ❀

"Wake up, Sprouties! It's the Flutterfly tryouts today!"

Lulu blinked open her eyes. Etta was flying backward around the room, wildly jingling a silver bell.

Coco, who was on Lulu's left, yawned and sat up. Next to Coco was Nova, stretching like a flower in sunlight. Zali, on Lulu's other side, was a small lump under her coverlet. "Can we sleep a little longer?" she mumbled.

"Nope," Etta said. "You're invited for breakfast in the Flutterfly branch. Come on, it smells delicious!"

The four Sprout Wings leapt out of bed in a flash. Even Zali! They pulled on their flying suits, feeling very excited. They couldn't wait to meet all the Flutterflies and see their branch.

Lulu and the others followed Etta up the spiraling stairs at top speed, passing many little doors on the way. Lulu longed to explore each and every branch, but there was no time.

Finally, Etta stopped at a cheerful yellow door and threw it open. "Here we are!"

"Welcome to Flutterfly!" called a big group of fairies dressed in yellow and blue.

The Flutterfly branch was much bigger than the Sprout Wings' one, and its walls were the rich brown of old growth. On the floor was plush blue carpet, dotted with yellow flowers. There were cozy armchairs, and fairy books floated in neat rows along the back wall. To one side was a pair of thick blue curtains.

"Come into the dining area," called one of the Flutterflies, opening the curtains with a flourish.

A long wooden table was all set up for breakfast. Blue cushions bobbed in midair before each place. Down the center of the table were trays covered in yellow cloths.

"We're having puff cakes with cloudberry sauce," said a fairy, pulling off the cloths to reveal trays and trays of little sponge cakes. The trays began hovering in the air. "The perfect thing to eat before the Flutterfly tryout."

"Why is that?" Lulu asked as they all gathered around the table, everyone hopping onto one of the floating cushions.

"Firstly, they're light," explained a tall boy fairy with dark hair. "So they're excellent for keeping you in the air."

"Secondly, they're delicious," Etta said, taking one as a tray floated past.

Lulu helped herself to a puff cake and took a bite. It was warm and soft—and oozing with cloud-berry sauce.

"This is the best thing I've ever tasted," Coco declared, reaching for another.

"I've never met a fairy who doesn't love a puff cake or three," Etta said.

"Have some morning dew tea," said a curly-haired Flutterfly, grabbing hold of a yellow teapot as it fluttered along the table. "So, did you all enjoy your first night in the Forever Tree?"

Lulu's nighttime adventure came flooding back.

She needed to talk to the others about it, but now was not the time. She took a gulp of tea and kept quiet.

"I slept so well," Zali said. She was clearly a champion sleeper.

"Same," Coco said. "It was good to stretch out after being curled up in my sprout flower."

"I had a lovely sleep, too," Nova said. "I feel as safe here as I did in my flower."

"That's because the Forever Tree is your home." Etta smiled at the little fairies.

There was the sound of tinkling bells. The Flutterflies began to chatter all at once.

"It's nearly time!"

"The tryout is starting soon!"

"Time to go, Sprouties," Etta said, hopping off her cushion. "The whole tree is excited."

"The whole tree?" Zali looked worried.

"Yes. All the Forever Fairies will be watching. We fairies love pod tryouts as much as we love puff cakes!"

The Sprout Wings glanced at one another. Lulu had a jumpy feeling in her chest. She was nervous, but more importantly, she had to warn the others about the trolls!

Before Lulu could utter a single word, Zali clutched her arm and groaned. "I'm soooo nervous! I don't think I'll do very well today."

"I'm nervous, too," Nova admitted shakily. "I'm not a very fast flyer."

Even confident Coco seemed worried.

Lulu looked at her friends' faces. She couldn't tell them about the trolls right now. It would only add to their jitters. They were nervous enough already!

It dawned on Lulu what she had to do instead: She must stay ahead of her friends on the adventure course, and keep an eye out for danger.

"Don't worry!" she assured the others, happy to have a plan. "We're all going to be great. Let's go do this adventure course!"

As Lulu, Nova, Coco, and Zali hurried down the curved stairs behind Etta—the musical notes now going lower instead of higher—a cheer erupted. The hall below was filled with excited, fluttering fairies. And they were all clapping and whooping for the Sprout Wings!

When they finally reached the bottom of the stairs, Etta flew through the crowd to meet them. She looked very different in a flowy yellow dress with a blue sash, and satin-blue slippers. Etta saw Lulu looking at her outfit and pulled a face. "The Forever Wings—our elders—say we must be in flounce wear for the tryouts."

"Flounce wear?" Zali giggled.

"That's what I call this formal stuff." Etta had to shout over the noise of jostling fairies. "Look!"

"'Go, Team Sprouties!'" Coco read the banner strung up high. "Awww, that is so sweet."

"We really are a team, aren't we?" Nova said thoughtfully.

"Of course we are! A great one!" Coco cried.

Lulu took a deep, happy breath and gathered her new friends in a group hug.

"Come on, Sprouties. Let's get out there." Etta led the way through the crowd. Fairies patted them on the back and called out encouragement as they passed.

"We'll be cheering for you!"

"You'll do great!"

As the Sprout Wings moved across the floor, Lulu felt a calm warmth rise from her feet up through her whole body. It was as if the tree itself was telling her that everything would be okay. It reminded Lulu of being folded inside her daffodil, safe and loved.

The heavy front door swung open and morning sunshine flooded in. Etta and the Sprout Wings rose above the crowd and over to the door. They each paused above the patch of moss at the entrance while the shoe spell was reversed. Their slippers disappeared and were replaced with flying shoes. Then they flew outside, where the morning air was warm and golden.

Lulu gazed up at the Forever Tree. Yesterday, it had been covered in tiny blooms of every color. Today, the branches were adorned with yellow and blue blossoms as big as pom-poms.

"The tree is wearing Flutterfly colors!" Zali clapped her tiny hands together.

Etta chuckled. "We say the Forever Tree has more outfits than any fairy who ever sprouted."

Shiny blue ribbons and yellow streamers hung all around them. Flags flapped in the breeze, the words GO, SPROUTIES! in gold letters.

More and more fairies flew out of the tree. Soon, the air was filled with their happy voices and flapping wings. The fairies flitted along the tree's generous branches, searching for the perfect viewing spot.

Close to the roots, a platform with four elegant chairs floated in midair. Sitting on the chairs were four equally elegant fairies.

They're like the Alpha Wings we met yesterday, Lulu

thought, *but older.* Their long hair was streaked with silver.

"The Forever Wings," Etta explained, sounding a little awed. "Our wise fairy elders. The fairy in pink and aqua is Sparkleberry. The Shimmerbud elder is in green and purple. Silver and gold are the Twinklestar colors. And you've probably guessed by now that the fairy in yellow and blue is Flutterfly."

"They look very important!" Nova said softly.

"They are! They judge the tryouts—and decide which new fairy goes into which pod," replied Etta. "Come!"

Lulu's stomach flipped. Nova was right. The fairies looked very important—and a little scary.

But as they approached the platform, the four elder fairies waved the Sprouties closer with warm smiles.

The Flutterfly elder's voice was rich and warm. "As you can probably imagine, today's tryout is particularly exciting for me. I just love watching each new season of Sprout Wings do the adventure course!"

The Shimmerbud elder leaned forward. "Do you have any questions?"

"I have one! What exactly do we have to do?" Coco asked.

Thank goodness Coco is always brave enough to speak up! thought Lulu.

"Good question! You must make your way from the base of the tree all the way to the top," the elder fairy said, pointing. "But this adventure course is not just about flying. There's also climbing and agility to consider. Remember, to be a Flutterfly, you must get around the forest quickly. You need to think fast when emergencies come up—and move even faster when help is needed."

"I guess we can't simply fly straight up the tree?" Coco asked.

"No! That wouldn't be much of a challenge for a fairy, would it?" The elder chuckled. "There are different stages. The first is stunt flying. Then comes the 'no-fly' stage, when you must walk on your hands along the length of a branch. Cartwheels are also welcome! Next, you need to catch the swinging vines from one side of the tree to the other. Finally, you'll wriggle up the hollow branches. Only when you've reached the very top of the Forever Tree will you be finished."

"Any other questions before we begin?" asked the Twinklestar elder.

"I have a question," Nova said slowly. "Can only one of us be chosen for the Flutterfly pod?"

Lulu's ears pricked up. She had been wondering the same thing.

"Not necessarily," said the elder in silver and gold. "Sometimes, two or more Sprout Wings might be picked for the same pod. But it's impossible to know which pod is right for which fairy until all the tryouts are complete. A fairy's talents can take time to show themselves."

Lulu felt even more excited than before. Maybe, just maybe, she and her new friends could all be in the same pod!

The Flutterfly elder clapped her hands. "Let us begin!"

The Sprout Wings waved goodbye to the elders as Etta ushered them to the starting point at the base of the tree. The judges' platform floated lower until it was hovering just above the ground.

"Good luck, Sprout Wings!" called fairies from all directions.

"Go, Sprouties!"

Etta pulled out her wand and gave it an elaborate swish. A glowing ribbon of light twirled out and began weaving its way up the branches of the tree.

"That is your guiding light," Etta explained. "It will show you the way."

The glowing ribbon curled around the trunk of the tree and looped over the lower branches. Lulu was still nervous. But the idea of flying along that curly path was thrilling!

Zali pulled a bundle from her pocket. "I made

bracelets for us all," she said, unwrapping it. "Yellow for Lulu, purple for Nova. This red one is for you, Coco. And mine is pink. They're our sprout flower colors."

"Zali! They're beautiful!" Coco said as the fairies slipped on their bracelets.

"Good luck, everyone," Nova said. "I might not be suited to Flutterfly, but I'm going to try my best."

"I think we'll all do fine," Coco said. "Especially you, Lulu! I can really imagine you as a Flutterfly."

The others nodded in agreement, and Lulu felt a wave of happiness. Oh, how she wanted to be a Flutterfly! But for the first time, Lulu realized that it might not be the right pod for the others.

"If we're in different pods," she said, her new worry tumbling out, "do you think we'll stay friends?"

The other Sprouties looked surprised.

"It doesn't matter which pods we're in, Lulu. We will always be friends," Nova said.

"It's going to take more than that to tear us apart!" Coco agreed, hands on hips.

"Really?" Lulu asked.

"Lulu," Zali said firmly, "fairies who sprout together are forever friends."

Lulu felt instantly lighter—and ready for the try-out! Whatever happened, she could handle it.

Etta raised her wand and began the countdown.

"Three, two, one . . . GO!"

Lulu shot into the air. Energy pulsed through her as she chased the guiding light. She zoomed around the massive trunk, following its twisty path.

"Great start, Sprout Wings!" cried the watching fairies.

Lulu glanced around, wondering if the trolls were watching. But she couldn't see any green faces in the crowd.

It felt good going fast. She could almost imagine she was racing through the forest on an important Flutterfly rescue mission. Lulu did one last loop of a branch and looked around for the guiding light. There it was!

"No-fly zone!" chanted the watching fairies. "Time for acrobatics!"

Instead of swirling around the branches, the light wiggled and jumped along the branches. Quickly, Lulu flipped onto her hands.

At first, she felt wobbly. But she soon found

her balance and began to walk along the branch. The more she did it, the easier it became—and she loved seeing the world upside down! The sky was above her feet, the ground below her head. Lulu walked on her hands for a bit, then swapped to cartwheels.

The watching fairies cheered and called out encouragement as the other Sprout Wings reached the no-fly zone. They began doing handstands and cartwheels along the branch behind Lulu.

At the end of the acrobatics section, Lulu saw that she had to leap up and catch hold of the branch above. Looking around, she noticed her friends were not far behind. They were doing so well! Lulu was

starting to tire a bit now, but she jumped as high as she could. Could she reach it? Yes! Lulu swung herself up and stopped to catch her breath.

Through the leaves, she spotted the judges' platform. It was rising as the Sprout Wings got higher up the tree.

Once more, Lulu looked around for the guiding light. It was just above her, swinging in midair! *What did that mean?* There were lots of vines dangling from the branch above. They were all different lengths and swayed in the breeze. Whenever the vines bumped, they lit up in the most magical colors.

"She's reached the Rainbow Vines!" called a boy fairy dressed in Flutterfly colors.

"Ooh, it's swing time. My favorite bit!" cried someone else from the crowd.

"Don't worry," said a voice Lulu recognized. Etta was hovering nearby. "The vines are strong. Use them to swing from one to another, until you get to the other side of the tree. There you'll find the hollow branches. You must squeeze through one—and then you'll be at the top!"

"That's great news!" said a tired-looking Coco, pulling herself onto the branch next to Lulu.

"Sure is," Nova puffed, appearing next.

Zali was close behind. The littlest fairy was too exhausted to speak at all!

Lulu was very pleased to see her friends and to be nearly at the finish line!

But she was also distracted. The branch they were on was strangely familiar—oh! This was where she had met Rox and Tex, the trolls! They had said the adventure course would be tricky. And sticky?

Lulu gave herself a shake. She just needed to fly ahead and look out for danger.

As a vine swung past, Lulu sprang up to grab it. She missed! *I'll get it next time*, she promised herself. And sure enough, when the vine swung back, Lulu jumped up and caught it easily. The vine turned bright purple and the watching fairies cheered.

Wheeeeee!

Riding on Rainbow Vines was the best feeling! Kicking with her legs, Lulu managed to swing across to the next vine and grab it with an outstretched hand. Yes! It turned orange. Then she swung to the next, which became blue. As she got the hang of it, Lulu began swinging faster from one rope to the next, gradually climbing higher.

Lulu could hear her friends swinging along behind her, the crowd calling out the colors as the vines were caught. *Red! Yellow! Pink!* She knew it must be beautiful, but she didn't dare look back for fear of missing the next vine.

Finally, there were only three vines to go. Beyond, Lulu could see a hollow branch. She was so close!

Lulu reached out for the next vine. As soon as she took hold of it, Lulu knew something was wrong. The others had been easy to grip. But this one was sticky and slippery. It was covered in something glowing and gooey! Lulu had flown ahead and found the danger, all right.

Glow honey! Lulu groaned as she lost her grip and began to fall . . .

Lulu tumbled through the air, too surprised to even flap her wings. But she didn't fall for very long. She just had time to think *Uh-oh!* before she landed on something soft and springy.

The watching crowd breathed a loud sigh. *Phew!*

Lulu bounced on the soft material, blinking in

confusion. What was going on? She looked around. She had landed in the middle of a beautiful spider-web. A very bouncy one!

"Lulu!"

"Are you okay?"

Lulu's friends were dangling from Rainbow Vines above. They all looked very worried.

"We're coming down to help!" Nova said.

"No, don't!" Lulu called. "I'm fine, just a little dizzy. You should stay safe and keep going!"

But Nova had already let go of her vine. She landed next to Lulu, causing them both to bounce up and down a few times.

Nova grinned. "My flower told me that spiderwebs are super strong. But I don't remember her saying they're bouncy. This is great!"

At that, Coco and Zali also dropped from their vines with loud squeals. They, too, landed on the spiderweb, grabbing Lulu's and Nova's hands as they did. Soon, all four Sprout Wings were jumping up and down together. It was even more fun than jumping on their beds!

The friends landed in a rumpled heap. Lulu pulled the other Sprout Wings into a hug. "You three are the best! I can't believe you left the adventure course to come check on me."

"Of course we did!" Nova said.

"We'd never just leave you here," Zali added.

Coco nodded. "We've done everything together since we sprouted. We're not going to stop now!"

Lulu felt a strange mix of feelings. She didn't know if she was going to laugh or cry. Maybe both! At that moment she knew for sure that their friendship could survive anything—even being in different pods.

"Plus, this web is fantastic," Zali declared, bouncing up and doing a somersault in the air.

"Of course it is," said a voice.

Two familiar green faces were peeping out at them through the leaves.

"Trolls!" cried Coco, Nova, and Zali.

Lulu crossed her arms. "Rox and Tex."

Coco shot her a surprised look.

"It was you two, wasn't it?" Lulu asked the trolls. "You put glow honey on that vine!"

"We sure did!" Rox said proudly. "It might be our best troll trick ever."

They high-fived.

"Someone could have been hurt." Lulu frowned.

"Chill, little fairy! You can all fly. Plus, we put this spiderweb here to catch you," Tex said.

"We added that after we met you last night. We like fairies who break the rules sometimes," Rox said.

"I'm confused." Zali looked at Lulu. "You've met these trolls?"

"We met Lulu when she snuck out last night. You were all asleep," Rox explained. "We had a good old chat, out there in the moonlight."

Coco smiled. "I wish I'd been there!"

"It's lucky no one saw you, Lulu," Nova said.

"Oh, we saw her," Etta said, appearing through the branches.

Lulu froze.

Etta looked stern, but a smile twitched at the corner of her mouth. "We'll talk about this later. Stick to the rules from now on, okay?"

Lulu nodded. "I promise!"

Then, to all the Sprouties' surprise, Etta bowed to the trolls and said, "I admit, that was a good trick." She turned back to the Sprout Wings. "Troll tricks are often annoying. But it's useful to know how Sprout Wings cope with the unexpected. That's an important part of being a Flutterfly. Now, remember, the adventure course isn't over yet!"

Lulu jumped to her feet and pulled up her

friends. "Etta's right, we need to finish! But hang on, how are we going to get back up there if we're not allowed to fly?"

"Shall we use the bouncy web?" Nova suggested.

"Great plan!" called Etta as she fluttered back into the crowd. "See you at the finish line!"

The Sprout Wings held hands.

"Ready?" Lulu asked.

"Ready!"

Together, the four fairies began to jump. Soon, they were almost as high as the vines. Then they were even higher.

On the next jump, Lulu spotted the guiding light on a high branch. "That's where we need to go!"

The Sprout Wings fell back down and bounced into the air again—and landed neatly on the branch, right next to the light.

"It's wriggle time!" called the watching fairies.

"You're close now, Sprouties!"

An excited buzz spread through the crowd and around the tree. Lulu felt charged and tingly. The guiding light had split into four paths, each one disappearing inside a hollow branch, which reached to the sky like the points on a crown. At the very top of each branch fluttered a yellow-and-blue flag.

Lulu couldn't wait to see the view! "See you up there!" she called, diving in.

Her nerves had disappeared, and all that was left was excitement. Lulu knew that if anything went wrong, her friends would help her out. Or maybe even the trolls would, in their own tricky way!

It was dark inside the hollow branch. Wriggling up it was difficult. Lulu had to push against the wood with her hands and feet. But it was also quite fun! Keeping her wings pressed to her back, she wriggled up the tunnel as quickly as she could.

Gradually, the light at the end of the hollow branch grew brighter. Then Lulu was right there, at the very end! It was a tight fit to squeeze through, but she squirmed until finally, she popped out.

Lulu was high above the treetops! The Magic

Forest stretched out in all directions. A second later, Nova, Coco, and Zali popped out of their branches, each fairy laughing and out of breath.

And as they did, hundreds of fairies surged up from the branches below, cheering, clapping, and doing excited midair loops.

"They've done it! The Sprout Wings have completed the adventure course!"

10

Etta whooshed up to them. "Congratulations!" she

cried with delight. "I didn't tell you earlier, but it's

quite rare for all four Sprout Wings to finish this

course. You did great!"

The Sprout Wings beamed. Lulu felt she might

burst with happiness. She was so proud of them all!

"Let's head back down," Etta said. "The elders would like to speak with you."

"I can hardly fly," groaned Zali.

"Same," said Coco. "Every bit of me is aching."

Etta smiled. "Sprout Wings are always pooped after the tryouts. You get to return in style! We've made you a flower carpet."

A group of fairies approached, each holding the edge of a rug woven from sweet-smelling grasses and brightly colored flowers.

"Climb aboard!" called the fairies.

The Sprout Wings stepped carefully onto the carpet. Secretly, Lulu wasn't even that tired. She almost wanted to do the course again, just for fun. But there was no way she was missing out on a flower carpet ride!

"It's like floating in a meadow." Zali sighed, stretching out. Coco and Nova lounged next to her and closed their eyes.

But Lulu sat cross-legged and gazed out at the forest. It was so beautiful—and so big!

This is home, Lulu told herself. *MY home.* She couldn't wait to explore every inch of it.

"Look, Lulu!" Etta pointed.

Lulu peeped over the edge. In front of the tree was a banquet table laden with cakes and cookies and other fairy treats. The goodies were all shaped like fairy wings and hovered just above the table. Prettily painted teapots and teacups were lined up, jiggling softly.

With a gentle bump, the carpet landed on the ground. Instantly, the grasses and flowers merged with the earth as if they had been growing there all along.

The crowd parted, forming a pathway to the grand table. At its head stood the four Forever Wings. The Flutterfly elder was holding a long, thin wooden box in her hands.

A hush fell.

"What's going on?" Coco whispered as the four friends inched toward the elder.

"Maybe we're about to find out who gets into Flutterfly?" Zali suggested.

Nova shook her head. "We only find out our pods after we've done all the tryouts, remember?"

"Nova is correct," said the elder. "The Pod Picking isn't until you've completed all four tryouts. You did wonderfully today, Sprout Wings. We're very impressed, aren't we?" She turned to the other elders, who nodded sagely. "It's not just that you all managed to finish the course. It's the way you supported one another. Working together is an important part of a Forever Fairy's life. Today we saw that you four are already doing that. Well done!"

Zali was so overcome by this praise that she

tried to hug her four friends at once. This was impossible for such a tiny fairy, and they all fell over. Everyone laughed—including the Forever Wings.

When the Sprout Wings had clambered to their feet again, the Flutterfly elder beckoned. "Please stand before me."

Holding hands, the Sprout Wings formed a line in front of the elegant fairy. She opened the wooden box. Nestled inside were four silver rods, glinting in the sunlight.

"Wands!" the Sprout Wings gasped in unison.

"Take one each," said the elder. "They are identical. A wand only changes when its fairy holds it."

Nova took one, followed by Coco and Zali. Lulu took a big breath and reached for hers. The wand felt cool at first, but warmth began spreading through it. And was her wand glowing brighter, too?

"Your wands are bonding with you," explained the elder. "Look closely—a fairy's wand tells the story of a life's journey."

As Lulu watched, an engraving appeared on her wand.

"A tiny pair of wings!" exclaimed Coco, staring at her own wand.

The Shimmerbud elder leaned in. "That is the Flutterfly symbol. Each time you successfully complete a tryout, that pod's symbol will appear on your wands. The next tryout is for my pod: Shimmerbud. Our symbol is a flower. That try-out will be about learning to heal the forest's creatures and working with nature."

"When do we start?" Nova asked, her eyes bright.

"Very soon." The Shimmerbud elder laughed. She was clearly pleased to see Nova's enthusiasm.

"You fairies have bonded with one another so well," Etta said. "Would you like to bond your wands as well? That means you'll always know when a bonded fairy is in need."

Lulu didn't think twice. Of course she wanted to always know when her friends needed her! She held her wand out, and the others did the same. When the four wands touched, a burst of stars and colorful light puffed into the air. It twinkled brightly and then floated away.

The four friends grinned at one another. Since sprouting, they'd done a lot together. Lulu knew there was still so much to discover about being a Forever Fairy—and she couldn't wait.

Turn the page for a special sneak

peek of Nova's fairy adventure!

All around, the forest was slowly coming to life. There were the low buzz of insects and the happy chirping of birds. Nova listened to their intricate songs. One bird in particular caught her attention. Its whistle was so happy, it made her want to dance! Nova pursed her lips and tried to copy the sound.

Not quite right . . . She tried again, and this time she was much closer!

Just then she heard someone else whistle. Looking about, Nova saw a creature sitting on a nearby branch. A troll! She had green hair tied into high bunches and dark-green freckles splashed across her green face. In fact, the only part of her that wasn't green was the very tip of her nose, which was pink.

The troll waved at Nova. "Early riser, huh? I'm the same. How can anyone lie in bed when there's a whole forest waiting to be explored? You're good at bird sounds. That's a gleebird you just imitated. I've been trying for ages to copy it. I'm Lex, by the way."

"I'm Nova," said Nova, fluttering over. "Mind if I join you?"

Nova wasn't normally chatty, but she was very excited to meet a troll. When she was growing in her flower, Nova had loved hearing stories about trolls. She knew they were a lot more mischievous than fairies, but they loved the Magic Forest just the same. Nova and the other Sprout Wings had already met a pair of trolls called Tex and Rox. But this troll was new and exciting and . . .

"Achoo!"

. . . unwell?

ABOUT THE AUTHORS

Maddy Mara is the pen name of Australian creative duo Hilary Rogers and Meredith Badger. Hilary and Meredith have been making children's books together for many years, including the Forever Fairies, Dragon Games, and Dragon Girls series. They love dreaming up new ideas and always have lots of projects bubbling away. When not writing, Hilary can be found cooking weird things or going on long walks, often with Meredith. And Meredith can be found teaching English online all around the world or daydreaming about being able to fly. They both currently live in Melbourne, Australia. Their website is maddymara.com.

DRAGON GIRLS

#1: Azmina the Gold Glitter Dragon

#2: Willa the Silver Glitter Dragon

#3: Naomi the Rainbow Glitter Dragon

#4: Mei the Ruby Treasure Dragon

#5: Aisha the Sapphire Treasure Dragon

#6: Quinn the Jade Treasure Dragon

#7: Rosie the Twilight Dragon

#8: Phoebe the Moonlight Dragon

#9: Stella the Starlight Dragon

#10: Grace the Cove Dragon

#11: Zoe the Beach Dragon

#12: Sofia the Lagoon Dragon

Collect them all!

DRAGON GAMES

PLAY THE GAME. SAVE THE REALM.

READ ALL OF TEAM DRAGON'S ADVENTURES!